When You Are
Least Expecting It . . .

Suddenly, a huge shadow crosses your path. You look up, but all you can see are some bumpy ridges that are wiggling. You look farther up and see two enormous legs. When you bend your neck all the way back, you see a gigantic head with one huge eye as large as a cantaloupe in the middle of the forehead.

This must be the Cyclops, you think, as the giant bends over and reaches his hand toward you.

Will you try to run from the Cyclops? Then turn to page 39! . . . Or, if you stay where you are and hope that it will not harm you, then turn to page 40!

WHICH WAY BOOKS #5

LOST IN A STRANGE LAND

R.G. Austin

Illustrated by
Lorna Tomei

AN ARCHWAY PAPERBACK
Published by POCKET BOOKS • NEW YORK

AN ARCHWAY PAPERBACK *Original*

 An Archway Paperback published by
POCKET BOOKS, a Simon & Schuster division of
GULF & WESTERN CORPORATION
1230 Avenue of the Americas, New York, N.Y. 10020

ISBN: 0–671–44110–8

First Archway Paperback printing April, 1982

10 9 8 7 6 5 4 3 2 1

For Mother and Tullos
with love

LOST IN A STRANGE LAND

Attention!

Which Way Books must be read in a special way. DO NOT READ THE PAGES IN ORDER. If you do, the story will make no sense at all. Instead, follow the directions at the bottom of each page until you come to an ending. Only then should you return to the beginning and start over again, making different choices this time.

There are many possibilities for exciting adventures. Some of the endings are good; some of the endings are bad. If you meet a terrible fate, you can reverse it in your next story by making new choices.

Remember: follow the directions carefully and have fun!

You are spending the summer in an isolated region of the Pacific Northwest. Your mountain cabin is located on the site of an ancient volcano, and your favorite activity is exploring the cavelike lava tubes that were formed thousands of years ago.

One day, as you are investigating the south side of the mountain, you see a small hole in the rocks. Upon careful inspection, you discover that the hole leads into a huge lava tube, the largest you have ever seen.

You ease your body through the small opening and climb inside. As you make your way through the darkness, you step carefully, uncertain of your footing.

Suddenly the ground beneath you begins to crack. The thin layer of lava gives way, and you feel yourself plunging through darkness and space.

(continued on page 2)

Soon, instead of falling, you begin to float. Hours later, you land softly on the ground.

Dazed, you look around. You can see very little; everything seems to be shrouded in mist. Ahead of you there is a giant billboard:

Beware: You are about to enter a world of fantastic creatures—from all times and all places, monsters and elves, dragons, witches and wizards. They have stepped out of their books, their tales, their songs. They are weird. They are wonderful. They are dangerous.

ENTER AT YOUR OWN RISK

Next to the billboard are three small signs, each pointing in a different direction.

If you go to Alphaland, turn to page 3.

If you go to Betaland, turn to page 4.

If you go to Gammaland, turn to page 5.

You have been walking for only a few minutes when you see a lovely young woman sitting under a tree. She is weeping.

"What is the matter?" you ask.

"My Stag," she says. "I have lost my beloved Stag."

"Perhaps I can help," you say. "Who are you?"

"I am a Vila, the Spirit of the Woods. Usually you can find me dancing or singing under the cherry trees. But now, I am helpless. I can go nowhere without my Stag and he has been stolen by the Ogre."

"I will get your Stag for you," you say. "Where is he being held?"

"He's somewhere in the Ogre's Hall," says the Vila. "But the only way to get into the Hall is to pass by the Hydra who guards the entrance."

You do not know what a Hydra is, but you are determined to free the Stag.

"Please," says the Vila, handing you a sword. "Take this. I fear you will need it."

Turn to page 7.

As you walk toward Betaland, the light grows dim. Undulating shadows darken your way, and you can barely see the path.

Suddenly, you hear a voice cry out, "Watch where you're going! You almost stepped on me."

You look down and see a tiny, wrinkled little man.

"Who are you?" you ask.

"A Pixie, of course," he answers indignantly. "What are you doing here?"

"I was exploring," you say. "And then I fell and . . . I was just looking for something different . . . an adventure, I guess."

"Well, you've certainly come to the right place. Betaland is filled with adventures. Treasures, too."

"I'd love to look for treasure."

"You have to be willing to risk your life," the Pixie says doubtfully.

"I'm willing to take that risk," you answer.

Turn to page 10.

You walk along a misty path for many hours. The fog is so thick that you can see nothing.

Finally, the fog disappears and you find yourself in front of a great gate made of glistening gold.

(continued on page 6)

You pass through the gate into a beautiful garden. Near the entrance to the garden are a huge banyan tree and a banquet table set with a fabulous array of food.

If you are tired and hungry and would like to sit down and rest beneath the tree, turn to page 17.

If you would prefer a quiet stroll in the garden, turn to page 18.

The Vila gives you directions, and you set out for the Ogre's Hall. Soon, you feel the ground grow soft beneath your feet. The mud oozes up around your ankles.

You are afraid that you will become stuck in the mire, and you are just about to turn back when you hear a terrifying roar.

(continued on page 9)

A huge lizardlike monster appears before you. The most horrifying aspect of the creature is that he has nine heads! You realize that this is the terrible Hydra.

If you think that you should kill the Hydra by cutting off his heads, turn to page 11.

If you feel that you cannot get close enough to the Hydra to cut off his heads, turn to page 12.

"The treasures," says the Pixie, "are the Hoard of Gold and the Serpent's Egg. The gold is guarded by Fafner, a venom-breathing dragon. If he breathes on you, his venom will enter your body in a matter of seconds. But . . . if you get past this monster, you will have untold riches for the rest of your life.

"The Serpent's Egg is guarded by the Medusa. She is a hideous-looking monster. Her head is covered with serpents, and all who look directly at her face turn to stone. But if you conquer her and carry out the Serpent's Egg, extraordinary powers—both physical and mental—will be yours forever." The Pixie pauses and looks at you carefully. "Are you willing to confront these dangers?"

"Yes," you answer.

"Then take this sword and magic shield with you. Guard them with your life."

If you set out in search of the gold, turn to page 13.

If you would rather have extraordinary powers, turn to page 14.

The monster moves toward you. You raise your sword and swing with all your strength.

The sword passes through the neck of one head. But as soon as the head falls to the ground, two more heads grow in its place.

You are horrified.

If you try to cut off the two new heads, turn to page 19.

If you suspect that the only way to defeat this monster is to cut off the center and largest head, turn to page 20.

You stand behind a tree and watch as the Hydra munches on clusters of purple blossoms. You realize that he is eating the blossoms of the Mandrake.

You know that the root of the Mandrake has been used for hundreds of years as an anesthetic and sleeping potion. You look around and spy some blossoms nearby, and you pull the entire plant out of the ground.

The roots are long and tubular. You strip the blossoms from them so that they look like carrots. Then you toss a bunch of roots to the Hydra.

All of the Hydra's heads seem delighted that they are being fed carrots. They nibble away at this unexpected delicacy. Soon the Hydra is fast asleep.

You run immediately into the tunnel. Once inside, you hear a sad moaning sound coming from the back of the tunnel.

Turn to page 45.

You say good-bye to the Pixie and set out for the gold.

The shadows grow darker, and soon you find yourself plunged into a darkness blacker than midnight. The glow of your shield casts a weak light on the path directly in front of you, but you are very frightened of what might be lurking in the dark.

Suddenly, a fire flares before you, and you are startled by its brightness.

> "Frog's feet and worm brains and a bit
> of spider's hair;
> Ant legs and snake skin and toenails
> from a bear."

You look to the side to see what kind of creature could be mumbling such an awful recipe, and you see a Witch stirring the contents of a huge caldron. You start to hide, but she sees you.

"Come, my dear and try my stew.

"You'll find it's tasty Witch's Brew," she says.

If you taste the brew, turn to page 21.

If you refuse to taste the brew, turn to page 22.

You are intrigued with the idea of having extraordinary powers. You would like to be stronger physically, of course, but you are especially eager to have extraordinary mental powers.

As you walk in the direction of the Serpent's Egg, a soft mist swirls in gray clouds around your body. You have been walking for more than an hour when suddenly the fog disappears and you find yourself at the edge of an inland sea.

There is a man swimming toward you; you wave to him. Immediately, he comes to you. When he steps out of the water, you are astounded to see that his body—from the waist down—is that of a horse.

(continued on page 16)

"Welcome," says the man-horse. "I am Nyk, the Spirit of the Sea. I am at your service. I will be happy to take you across the water on my back," he says. "Or, if you would like to see my kingdom under the sea, I would be honored to have you as my guest."

If you want to cross the sea immediately and continue your search for the Serpent's Egg, turn to page 23.

If you would rather see the water kingdom than search for the Serpent's Egg, turn to page 24.

You fill your platter with grapes and other fresh fruit, and you sit in the shelter of the banyan tree.

Soon, you grow sleepy, and you take a nap. When you awaken, you feel refreshed.

"Are you feeling better now?" says a voice.

You look around but see no one.

"Who is that?" you ask.

"Me, of course. Who else?" says the tree. "It's been eons since anyone enjoyed the comfort of my branches. The Cyclops used to come visit me all the time, but lately he has been too busy protecting his gold."

"Where is this gold?" you ask.

"On the other side of the tulip bed," says the tree. "The Cyclops keeps it all to himself. He never shares it with anyone."

"You must be lonely," you say.

"Sometimes," says the tree. "I miss Mab, the Fairy Queen. She used to visit me, too. But she hasn't been here in weeks. She won't leave the lilac grove. I'm worried about her."

If you seek the Cyclops' gold, turn to page 25.

If you go to see Mab in the lilac grove, turn to page 26.

You stroll through the garden, taking various turns and twists in the path. You are constantly surprised at how many paths there are. When you brush against one of the thick, high bushes bordering the path, your skin is cut by a thorn. You look at the bushes carefully, and you realize that they are covered with sharp thorns.

You turn to go back; but after wandering for several hours, you realize that you are hopelessly lost in a maze.

Suddenly, you hear a snorting and stomping noise. You run from the threatening sound until you come to a fork in the path.

If you take the path to the right, turn to page 27.

If you take the path to the left, turn to page 28.

You realize that the Hydra is a cumbersome beast who moves very slowly. His heads, however, are in constant motion, and you have difficulty getting close enough to strike.

Finally, you maneuver into position. With one swift slash of the sword, you sever the two new heads. In their places, four heads spring up.

Turn to page 29.

You move close to the Hydra and swing your sword at the middle head. You miss and nick one of the side heads, making the Hydra very angry.

He lunges for you and barely misses. You decide that this plan is too dangerous and devise a new strategy.

Turn to page 30.

You take a cup of Witch's Brew and drink it in one gulp.

Immediately, your head begins to spin, and you are temporarily blinded. And then, to your horror, you see hideous creatures all around you where there were none before.

"Now you have a new kind of vision," cackles the Witch. "For Witch's Brew gives the drinker night-sight."

All around you there are grotesque creatures of the night that slither and crawl and slide toward you.

If you pretend that you do not see the creatures and slowly walk on, turn to page 32.

If you run like crazy, turn to page 33.

You pretend for a moment that you are going to drink the Witch's Brew. And then, without warning, you start to run.

"Catch the Earthling!" cries the Witch. "Don't let it get away!"

You continue to run as fast as you can. Just when you think you are safe, you trip and fall down a steep incline.

Turn to page 48.

"I must warn you," Nyk says. "There are beautiful creatures called Sirens who inhabit an island in the middle of this sea. They make such enticing and magical music that few can resist their call. Once you are drawn to them, you will stay on their island forever and listen to the music that makes you forget all things. Eventually, you will starve, for even food becomes unimportant."

"I cannot imagine that music could be that powerful," you say.

"Nevertheless," says Nyk, "you may want to wrap this rope around yourself while I hold on to the other end. That way, you can be certain that you will not be lured by the Sirens."

If you wrap yourself in the rope, turn to page 35.

If you think you can resist the music, turn to page 36.

You climb onto Nyk's back, and he slowly descends beneath the water. You are thrilled to feel yourself extracting oxygen from the water, as though you had gills.

If you want to tour the underwater kingdom, turn to page 37.

If you want to visit Nyk's castle, turn to page 38.

You run down a path bordered by yellow and red and orange tulips. The sun is shining, and it is a lovely day. You think that this is a lark of an adventure to be embarking upon.

Suddenly, a huge shadow crosses your path. You look up, but all you can see are some bumpy ridges that are wiggling. You look farther up and see two enormous legs. When you bend your neck all the way back, you see a gigantic head with one huge eye as large as a cantaloupe in the middle of the forehead.

This must be the Cyclops, you think, as the giant bends over and reaches his hand toward you.

If you try to run from the Cyclops, turn to page 39.

If you stay where you are and hope that the Cyclops will not harm you, turn to page 40.

As you approach the lilac grove, you are surrounded by the sweet smell of the purple and white blossoms. The birds sing happily, and everything seems perfect until you reach Mab, the Fairy Queen.

She is sitting on a blossom with her head on her knees, crying.

"What is it?" you ask.

"My tapestries," she says. "Every day I weave dreams into my tapestries. Without my tapestries, no one would have dreams. I work hard to make them beautiful so that everyone in the world will awaken happy and refreshed. But every night someone is ruining the tapestries. When my work is destroyed, the dreams turn into nightmares. I do not know who is doing this or why."

If you stay up all night to see if you can discover who is destroying the tapestries, turn to page 41.

If you build a trap to catch the wrongdoer, turn to page 42.

You run down the path to your right, frantic to get away from the horrible-sounding noises. You run into a dead end.

When you turn around, your way is blocked by a terrible monster. His head is that of a bull, but he has the body of a man.

"Food for the Minotaur!" cries the monster as he moves toward you. His breath is foul and his eyes are a fiery red. There is nothing you can do. You are trapped.

The End

You run down the left path, frantic to escape from the terrible noise. Finally you stop and listen. You can no longer hear the noise, but you know that you must go on.

If you think you would be less conspicuous if you get down close to the ground and crawl, turn to page 43.

If you continue running, turn to page 44.

As you move away from the Hydra, you get an idea. If you can lure the beast away from the entrance, you might be able to run past him into the Ogre's Hall.

Making believe that you have tripped, you fall to the ground and cry out in pain. You grasp your ankle and writhe on the ground.

The cumbersome monster moves away from the entrance toward you. You have no doubt that he will tear you apart if he gets to you.

When the Hydra is just a few feet away, you stand up and run. The monster does not move swiftly enough, and you race to the entrance without being touched.

Once inside, you realize that you are in a long, dark tunnel. There is a torch on the wall, and you take it in your hand.

Ahead of you are two paths. From one you hear a strange moaning sound.

From the other, you hear the music of flutes.

If you move in the direction of the moaning, turn to page 45.

If you move in the direction of the music, turn to page 46.

The Hydra lunges again, but this time you are ready. You swing up onto a tree branch so that you can strike at the Hydra from above. With one swift move, you sever the Hydra's center head.

Without waiting to see what happens, you leap from the tree and run into the tunnel. In no time, you emerge, riding on the back of the liberated white Stag.

The Stag flies through the marsh. You look back and see the Hydra lying motionless on the ground.

When the Vila sees you, she bursts into tears of joy as she throws her arms around the neck of her Stag.

(continued on page 31)

"I wish to show my gratitude to you with all the powers at my command," she says. "I can send you home now, if that is your desire. Or, if you wish to explore our world further, I can arrange for a fantastic tour. You must choose now, for soon I must be gone."

If combating the Hydra was enough for you, and you wish to return to your family and friends, you may end the story here.

The End

If, however, you wish to explore further, turn to page 47.

You know that these terrible creatures have not harmed you up until this point, so you pretend that they are still invisible. You hope that they will ignore you.

You look straight ahead and start to walk. Hideous screams and shrieks surround you. You feel slimy claws and sticky tongues on your skin, but you continue to walk, pretending that they are not there.

Just when you think that you have left this nightmare behind, you trip and stumble down a steep incline.

Turn to page 48.

You run, clutching your shield and sword as you dodge in and out of the hideous creatures. You swipe at them with your sword, but they are too swift for you and they jump away. There seems to be no end to the monsters of the darkness.

(continued on page 34)

Finally, you see a glimmer of light ahead. You rush toward it with all your strength. But, before you can escape the dark, the creatures surround you. They laugh hysterically as they clutch at you with their claws.

There is nothing you can do. You belong to them now. Soon you will become one of the creatures of the night.

The End

Nyk helps you wrap the rope around your body, and then you climb onto his back. The water of the inland sea is crystal clear and just cool enough to be refreshing without chilling you.

Soon you hear the song of the Sirens. It comes to you in waves, the most beautiful, the most enticing music you have ever heard. You struggle to climb off Nyk's back and swim toward the music. You are overwhelmed with the thought that life is not worth living if you cannot be surrounded by this incredible music forever. But the rope holds fast against your struggle, and soon the song fades into a lovely memory.

When you are standing on land again, Nyk says to you, "If you still wish to search for the Serpent's Egg, go in the direction of the setting sun. But I must warn you: many people have gone in search of this fabulous egg. But none—not one—has ever returned."

Turn to page 49.

"I shall go without the rope," you say. "For there is no music that could lure me to my death."

"As you wish," says Nyk. "Climb onto my back."

Soon you are in the middle of the sea. It is then that you hear it: the most beautiful, the most enchanting music you have ever heard. Surely, it is not of this world, you think. Those who make music so exquisite cannot be evil.

You jump from Nyk's back and swim toward the Sirens. There are several of them sitting on a tiny island.

They welcome you with smiles and songs as you climb up beside them. You have never felt so blissful in your entire life, and you are certain that you have found the answer to all things.

If you sing along with the Sirens, turn to page 51.

If you ask the Sirens about their music, turn to page 52.

You float on Nyk's back as he swims languidly through the warm, crystal clear water. Suddenly, a great shadow looms over you, and the entire undersea world turns dark.

"What is happening?" you ask.

"Look up," says Nyk.

You look. There is a shimmering in the water. Then you see the underbelly of a gigantic sea serpent, her tail trailing in a relaxed manner through the water.

"Is it safe to be here?" you ask.

"Of course," says Nyk. "It's only Nessie. Do you want to meet her?"

If you want to meet Nessie, turn to page 54.

If you decide that encountering a sea monster is a bit too forbidding, turn to page 56.

You swim on Nyk's back toward the castle. You have never seen anything lovelier in your life. There are turrets and towers and even a moat. The water in the moat is dark and murky, in contrast to the clarity of the sea. As you approach the castle, a huge drawbridge is lowered. You and Nyk cross the bridge.

Suddenly Nyk stops. "Something is wrong," he says. "When I left, the front door was open. I have always trusted the creatures of the sea to take care of the castle when I am gone, for it belongs to all of us, even though I am the king. If the door is closed, it means someone is there who does not belong."

"But you are the king," you say. "Surely no creature would harm you."

"There is only one creature in the sea against whom I cannot defend myself."

"Who is that?" you ask, a shiver of fear traveling down your spine.

"The giant Octopus," he says.

Turn to page 58.

You do not like the looks of this horrible character, so you run between his feet and hide behind a rock. You are so tiny that he does not see you.

The earth shakes as the Cyclops walks past you. You stay hidden until the tremors stop, and then you run as fast as you can in the other direction. Soon you are confronted by a huge, iron fence.

Turn to page 59.

You stand trembling. The hand picks you up and raises you . . . you are staring into the horrible single eye.

"You look like a tasty morsel," the Cyclops says in a booming voice.

"Who, me?" you say. "Look," you continue, pinching your arm and sucking in your stomach. "There's no fat on me. I'd be tough and hard to chew."

"Then I'll just have to fatten you up!" says the Cyclops.

He places you in an iron cage next to his treasure of gold. Then he plies you with grapes and apples and all manner of good food.

"I only eat junk food," you say. "That's all."

"Junk food? What's that?"

"Oh, hamburgers with catsup and pickles, and french fries and hot dogs and hot-fudge sundaes. That sort of thing."

Soon you are surrounded with junk food.

If you pretend to eat the food and then try to hide it, turn to page 61.

If you eat the food, turn to page 62.

Mab sits beside you in the dark. You talk and sing together in your efforts to stay awake. But soon Mab falls asleep, and you do not want to disturb her. You cover her with a leaf and let her sleep.

You do not see the funny little man creep up behind you.

Turn to page 63.

You work together to dig a deep hole. Then you cover the hole with branches. Whoever steps on the branches will fall right into the hole.

"All right," you say. "Now, let's put the tapestry behind the trap."

Then you both go to sleep.

In the middle of the night, you hear a crash and a rumpus and a terrible scream.

If you rush immediately to the trap, turn to page 64.

If you decide to go back to sleep and investigate in the morning, turn to page 65.

You begin to crawl. You have not traveled far when you meet a tiny gray mouse.

"Are you lost?" squeaks the mouse.

"I sure am!" you whisper. "And I keep hearing this terrible noise."

"Oh. That must be the Minotaur. You are right to fear him. The Minotaur is a horrid creature with the head of a bull and the body of a man. And he eats every creature he can get hold of. I'm lucky, of course. I'm small enough to scurry under the bushes when he's around."

"What can I do?" you ask.

"Follow me," he answers. "I'm an old hand at mazes. I'll show you the way out."

Turn to page 67.

You take one turn after another, trying to remember where you have been. But everything looks the same. You take one more path and discover a group of people huddled together in a corner near a cluster of tall reeds. They look up in fear when you approach them.

"You, too?" you whisper.

They nod, too frightened to speak.

"Why haven't you done anything?" you ask.

"We're helpless against such a beast," they answer. "There's nothing we *can* do. He intends to eat us all when he finds us."

Turn to page 69.

As you travel down the tunnel, the moans grow louder. You cannot tell whether the sounds are human or animal.

When you come to the end of the path, there is a small barred door directly in front of you. You look inside and you see the Stag. He is so white that his coat shines in the dim light.

You slip the bolt on the door and step inside.

If you lead the Stag out of the cell into the tunnel, turn to page 70.

If you climb on his back, turn to page 71.

The music grows louder and more joyous as you near the end of the tunnel. When you reach the very end, there are two doors. The music sounds as if it is coming from both of them.

If you open the door on the right, turn to page 72.

If you open the door on the left, turn to page 73.

You tell the Vila that this fantastic world is too exciting to leave until you have seen everything you can.

Then the Vila sings a mystical, haunting song as she dances gracefully around the cherry tree.

Before she has finished the song, a gigantic bird swoops down from the sky.

"This is a Roc. He will be your guide," the Vila explains.

You have never seen a bird so spectacular. His beauty fills you with awe. He is pure white, except for the golden tips of his wings and the red crown on his head.

"Your wish is my command," the Roc says to you. "Would you like to go to the Midsummer Night's Festival, or would you like to visit the Sphinx?"

If you choose to go to the Midsummer Night's Festival, turn to page 75.

If you would prefer a visit to the Sphinx, turn to page 76.

"Aha!" says a little voice at the bottom of the hill. "At last we've caught ourselves a Witch!"

"I'm no Witch," you protest.

"So, you're not," says a tiny Leprechaun. "What are you doing here?"

"I'm searching for the Hoard of Gold that is guarded by the Fafner."

"Good," says the little man. "When you kill the Fafner, you can bring us back his teeth."

"What are you going to do with the dragon's teeth?" you ask.

"Plant them, of course. Everyone knows that for every dragon's tooth you sow, ten warriors spring out of the soil. The Leprechaun kingdom is in danger of being wiped out by the Witches. We desperately need warriors to protect us. I will make you a deal. I will lead you to the lair of the Fafner, if you will bring us back his teeth to sow."

If you accept the deal, turn to page 77.

If you are convinced that the task before you is difficult enough, without having to yank out the dragon's teeth too, turn to page 78.

You thank Nyk for his warning, but you are convinced that the treasure of the Serpent's Egg is worth the risk.

Then you set off. Soon you come to a cave from which a foul, rancid odor drifts past you. You hear a loud hissing inside, as if the cave is inhabited by thousands of snakes; and you know that this must be the home of the Medusa who guards the Serpent's Egg.

If you try to lure the Medusa out of the cave, turn to page 79.

If you go inside the cave in search of the Medusa, turn to page 81.

You begin to sing with the Sirens and feel yourself drawn into the song. You feel as if you are suspended in perfect bliss, and you want to stay with the Sirens forever. Not even the need for food could make you leave now.

The End

"Your music is lovely," you say to the Sirens.

But they do not answer. They just continue to sing.

"When do you stop singing?" you ask. But the only answer is the song.

Suddenly, you know that they will never stop, that they will sing forever in order to keep you there. You are so frightened that you begin to scream; you realize that, as long as you are screaming, you do not hear the Sirens' song.

(continued on page 53)

You continue to scream as you dive under the water, where you cannot hear any sounds. You swim as far as you can; and when you come up for air, you scream again. You do this until you reach the far shore where you can no longer hear the music.

Stepping up on the land, you realize that you have lost your sword and shield somewhere along the way. You know that you cannot seek the Serpent's Egg without them.

You walk sadly along the shore of the sea until you come to a fork in the road.

If you take the road to the right, turn to page 82.

If you take the road to the left, turn to page 83.

You swim slowly upward until you are face to face with the sea monster. Her golden scales sparkle in the blue water. Surprisingly, she has a gentle and welcoming expression on her face.

"Who are you?" asks Nessie.

"A tourist, of sorts," you answer.

Just then, Nessie begins to blink her eyes and wiggle her head. "Oh, no!" she says.

"What's the matter?"

"I have this itch behind my right gill, and it's driving me crazy."

(continued on page 55)

You reach up and scratch her gently. You feel a small fish lodged in a corner of the gill, and you extract it. As you lift up the fish, a transparent golden scale falls off in your hand.

"You did it!" cries Nessie. "The itch is gone!"

"But I am afraid that one of your beautiful scales came off in my hand," you say.

"Keep it," Nessie says. "I've got plenty."

"I have a question," you say to Nessie.

"Shoot."

"By any chance, are you the Loch Ness monster?"

Turn to page 57.

"I think it might be too dangerous," you tell Nyk. "Is there any risk?"

"Of course," says Nyk. "Nessie is very large. There is always the chance that you will get hit with a flipper or banged with her tail. She can be forgetful, too. Once I saw her swallow someone because her mouth was open and she wasn't paying attention. That's the way it is. There's a risk in almost everything we do."

"Well, this is one risk I don't think I want to take," you say.

Without another word, Nyk takes you back to the surface and deposits you on shore.

"Isn't there more?" you ask.

"Not for someone unwilling to explore, to risk," Nyk says sadly.

Suddenly Nyk is gone, and you know that you will wonder for the remainder of your life about the sea serpent and the adventures you might have had.

The End

"Yes, indeed," Nessie says. "That's what they call me."

You realize that you are holding in your hand the only positive proof that the Loch Ness monster exists.

If you want to hurry home so that you can show everyone your golden scale, turn to page 84.

If you want to learn more about Nessie, turn to page 85.

You swim with Nyk to a window and peer inside the castle. Nothing you have ever imagined has prepared you for the awesome size and bulk of this gigantic creature. His tentacles are as long as a football field; his lump of a body, the size of a house.

"He has captured the castle," Nyk says. "I do not know how we will ever get him out. Perhaps we should leave and see if we can find help."

If you leave with Nyk, turn to page 86.

If you devise your own plan to evict the Octopus, turn to page 89.

You go around the fence. When you reach the other side, a vast arid land stretches before you. The trees and plants are dry and wilted. The animals are quiet. There is no song from the birds of the forest.

There are few people; and when you meet them, they only nod, as if they are too weary and too hungry to speak.

Finally, you meet a woman who tells you that her land has not had rain for two years. Her people are starving. She also tells you that their only hope is to get food and water from the people who live in the Bower of Bliss.

(continued on page 60)

"We have been told that they are kind people," she says. "But they do not seem to know that we exist. The Bower of Bliss," she tells you, "is sweet and fruitful; the nightingale's song floats on the warm summer breeze. The food is plentiful, and the water is sweet."

"Why don't you go there?" you ask.

"Because the only way to get there is either to steal the Cyclops' treasure or to cross the Lake of Boiling Blood. We are too weak to do those things," she says. "Will you go tell them of our plight?"

"Of course," you answer.

If you try to steal the Cyclops' gold, turn to page 90.

If you try to cross the Lake of Boiling Blood, turn to page 91.

When the Cyclops is gone, you take the food and throw it out of the cage. Soon the cage is surrounded by birds picking away at the food.

At the end of the day, the Cyclops returns.

"Are you fat yet?" the hideous giant asks.

You start to speak, but he interrupts. "What is that funny smell?" he asks, sniffing the air.

You try to ignore all the food on the ground that the birds did not eat. But the giant sees it.

"It's spoiled food! How dare you! Did you think you could get away with that?"

The giant opens the door of the cage and picks you up. You are so frightened you cannot speak.

"I don't care whether you are fat or not! So you'll be a snack instead of a meal."

The End

You take a bite of the hamburger as the Cyclops watches.

"Umm," you say, licking your lips. "Delicious. Want a bite?"

The giant takes the hamburger and pops it into his mouth.

Then you take the ice-cream cone and lick it. "Terrific!" you say. "Mocha peanut butter. Want a taste?" And the Cyclops swallows the whole cone.

Bit by bit, the Cyclops eats hundreds of hamburgers, mountains of ice cream, and thousands of chocolate-chip cookies. By the end of the third day, you have lost a lot of weight, and the giant is fat and happy and sleepy.

Finally, the Cyclops falls asleep. When he is snoring, you discover that you are so thin that you can slip between the bars, right out of the cage.

Then you tiptoe to the treasure chest and fill a huge bag with gold. You are pleased with yourself when you think of all the people who will be saved because you will buy them food and shelter and clothing.

The End

He reaches into his pouch and gathers some fine gold dust in his hand. Then, when you are not looking, he sprinkles the dust in your eyes.

As you drift slowly into sleep, the sweet song of the nightingales fills the air.

Later, you awaken with a scream.

"What is it?" Mab asks, rubbing her eyes.

"I just had a horrible nightmare," you tell her.

"Well, we missed catching the culprit," Mab says sadly. "I think we'd be better off with a trap."

Turn to page 42.

It is the middle of the night, and you cannot see a thing. But you can hear noises at the bottom of the hole. You do not know what to do.

Turn to page 93.

Soon the harsh noise subsides, and the song of the night birds fills the air. You and Mab drift into sleep.

Suddenly, you are awakened again by a terrible nightmare. It is nearly dawn, and you decide to peek inside the trap.

"It's about time," says a little wizened Leprechaun. "What the heck do you think you are doing, building a trap like this for me to fall into! I'll make you pay for this!"

"So you're the one who's been destroying the tapestries of dreams," you say. "It's you who will pay."

(continued on page 66)

"Me? You think I'd do such a thing? You gotta be kidding. Neither I nor my children have had a decent night's sleep in weeks. We're so cranky, all we do is fight. I came here to talk to Mab about this. I'm not the one who's making trouble."

"Oh," you say, a little embarrassed.

"Tell you what I'm gonna do," says the Leprechaun. "I'm gonna climb up in that tree there, and I'm not gonna come down until I catch the destroyers of dreams."

The Leprechaun hops up into the tree, and you hear a scream of surprise.

"Take a look at this, would ya!"

You peer into the branches and see the most beautiful nests you have ever seen. They are constructed of colorful, shining threads, the very threads of the tapestries.

The Leprechaun awakens the nightingales and screams at them.

"But we didn't know we were doing anything wrong!" the birds protest.

When Mab discovers what has happened, she says, "I have an idea. From now on, I'll leave my scraps of yarn and thread for you. Your nests will still be beautiful, but we will have sweet dreams again."

And that is exactly what she did. And everybody was happy.

The End

You follow the mouse through so many twists and turns that your head is spinning. Finally, you see an exit.

You thank the mouse and are just about to leave when a horrible creature steps out in front of you.

"Not so fast, my friend," says the Minotaur.

"Oh, no," says the mouse. Then he whispers to you, "Be ready to run."

In a daring move, the mouse runs up the Minotaur's leg and then starts running in circles around the monster's belly.

"Hey!" yells the Minotaur. "That tickles!" In his frantic efforts to rid himself of this ticklish nuisance, the Minotaur turns away from you. Without hesitating, you run past the monster and out into the open toward the banyan tree and freedom.

You look back just in time to see the mouse scurry down the monster's leg and run into the bushes.

The End

"There is strength in numbers," you tell the group. "Never forget that. There are twenty of us and only one Minotaur. Here's the plan." Then you explain it to them.

Together you pick the tall reeds that line the paths of the maze next to the thorny bushes. It takes you several hours to braid them into long, strong rope.

"Now we wait," you say. "Stay huddled together as if you are frightened."

Eventually, the Minotaur finds you. He approaches the group, licking his chops.

"Now!" you yell. And everyone in the group, working together, rushes the Minotaur and attacks him. Soon he is tied up, with the rope wound around him hundreds of times.

"Now, let's get out of here," you say. "Sooner or later, if we work together, we'll find the exit."

"Thank goodness you came!" says the group. "You have saved our lives."

The End

You lead the Stag out of the cell and begin to walk toward the exit. The Stag hurries, but you cannot keep up with his nimble steps, and he is forced to slow down for you.

Suddenly, there is a horrible growling noise. You start to run, but you are too slow.

From out of the shadows steps the most hideous Ogre you could imagine. He is a giant, covered with black, matted hair. His eyes glow red; his lips are a purple, liverish color. He reaches his huge, hammy hands toward you. But before the Ogre can grab you, the Stag picks you up in his mouth and gallops through the exit. Soon you are the co-guest of honor at a sumptuous welcome-home banquet for the Stag.

The End

The Stag remains still as you climb on his back. You are surprised at how comfortable you feel.

With a nod of his noble head, he steps out of the cell into the tunnel and begins to run. His movements are so swift that you feel as if you are flying.

When you get to the end of the tunnel, you see the Hydra waiting for you. But the Stag is not deterred. He leaps over the monster with perfect grace and carries you through the marshes back to the Vila.

When she sees you, the Vila cries out with joy.

Then she turns to you and speaks in her beautifully musical voice. "It is in my power to grant you one wish. I hope in that way to repay you for your kindness and valor."

Without hesitating, you say, "I would like to return home."

"Anytime you wish," she answers with a smile.

The End

You open the door on the right and peek inside. The room is dark. Holding your torch high, you step inside.

You are in a tiny cell. You cross the room and look through the window on the other side.

Suddenly, you hear a loud crash and you turn around. The door behind you has shut; you hear the bolt slipping into place.

You rush to the window. When you look out, you find yourself staring into the face of a hideous, gigantic Ogre.

"Aha!" he says, licking his lips. "I see that I have caught myself some dinner!"

The End

You open the door carefully and peek into the room. All you can see are five little Pixies playing flutes. You are so enchanted by the music that you step inside.

"Play!" roars a voice from the end of the room.

You look in the direction of the voice and see a huge Ogre. When he sees you, he asks, "And do you play music, too? My Pixies, here, are wonderful, don't you think?"

You look at the Pixies and notice that they are chained together, prisoners of the Ogre.

"You, too, must play for me," orders the Ogre.

You do not know how to play a flute, but you wonder if you should fake it.

If you tell the Ogre that you will play for him, turn to page 94.

If you offer, instead, to teach the Ogre how to dance, turn to page 95.

You have always wanted to fly, and you are ecstatic when the Roc picks you up gently in his talons and swoops into the sky. You think that this is the most exhilarating feeling you have ever experienced.

Off into the golden light you fly; but soon, you enter darkness.

"We have just entered the Land of Light," says the Roc, totally confusing you. "For one day a year, there is darkness in the Land of Light. During the darkness, the Elves light bonfires and dance in celebration of Midsummer Night. If the dancing is joyful, the light returns the next day."

You look below and see hundreds of bonfires flickering in the darkness. When the Roc lands, you are surrounded by thousands of dancing Elves who are happily celebrating Midsummer Night.

If you wish to join the Elves in their dance, turn to page 98.

If you think that this is a childish celebration, and you would rather explore the edges of the night, turn to page 100.

The Roc picks you up in his talons and lifts you effortlessly into the sky. You are elated by the feeling of flying and are vaguely disappointed when the bird sets you down in the light, sandy desert.

When you look up, your disappointment turns to fear. An enormous monster is staring into your eyes.

Turn to page 101.

The Leprechaun leads you around three mountains before you reach the lair of the Fafner. Finally, the little man tugs on your shoelace and says, "We have arrived. The Fafner will be around the next bend. Here is a bag to hold the dragon's teeth. I wish you luck, and I will wait for you at home."

You walk around the bend, and there you see one of the most fearsome creatures imaginable. A foul stench drifts from his mouth, and his eyes are blood-red. The scales on his back are crawling with maggots, and his claws are filthy with slime.

You try to sneak up on the Fafner. Just as you are coming within the area in which he can zap you with his venomous breath, the Fafner sees you and turns in your direction.

If you stand your ground and hope that you can outmaneuver the Fafner, turn to page 102.

If you climb the tree off to one side of the dragon, in the hope that you can get out of range of his breath, turn to page 104.

You thank the Leprechaun but explain that you have enough of a task before you without having to pull out the teeth of a dragon.

You move on, holding the shield in front of you for protection.

Soon you know that you are near the Fafner's lair because the air is filled with a horrid odor.

You walk slowly, watching for the dragon. You do not think that the Fafner would be clever enough to allow you to pass so that he could sneak up behind you. But that is exactly what he does.

You feel a fiery burning on your legs and back, and you know that the Fafner has breathed his deadly venom on you.

The End

Very quietly, you set about gathering sticks and small branches. You pile them near the entrance to the cave. Then you rub two sticks together until they spark. Soon you have a fire burning.

Using your shield, you fan the smoke into the cave. Soon you hear a scurrying noise, and you assume that it is the Medusa running from the smoky cave.

You know that you will turn to stone if you look directly at her face, so you stand near the entrance with your back to the mouth of the cave. Holding your shield in front of you, you wait for the Medusa's reflection to appear in the shield.

You hear coughing as she emerges. In your shield you see the snakes writhing on her head. You can barely even look at the horrible face reflected in the shield.

Still using your shield as a mirror, you back toward her. She does not see you, for she is rubbing her smoke-filled eyes. Quickly, you raise your sword and lop off her terrible head.

(continued on page 80)

You hear snakes hissing and writhing on the ground. Then the sound stops. Using your shield as a guide, you reach behind you and grab the head. Then, without ever looking at the face, you walk to the sea and fling this horror into the deep water.

You hurry back into the cave and go inside. At the back of the cave there is an unearthly glow, as if a mysterious light has grown from nothingness. In the center of this light is an egg that is the size of a small watermelon.

You pick up the egg slowly and return to the sunlight. Even there, the egg competes with the sun in its brightness.

You are standing at the cave's entrance admiring the egg when you hear a scurrying and scuttling noise behind you. Turning to see the source of this noise, you are horrified to see a multitude of red-eyed rats coming toward you.

If you are terrified and lift the egg to throw it at the rats, turn to page 106.

If you think that you can outrun the rats, turn to page 107.

You creep up to the entrance of the cave and peek inside. It is pitch black, and you cannot see a thing. *If I cannot see anything,* you think, *then I cannot see the Medusa*. Therefore, being near her cannot turn me to stone.

Carefully, you step inside the cave. You move slowly, clutching your sword and shield as you make your way into the darkness.

You feel the floor of the cave slant downward as you descend deeper and deeper. The foul odor grows stronger. You cannot see a thing.

Suddenly, there is a flare of light. Oh, no! you think. The Medusa has lit a match. Then you see the most hideous face you have ever seen. You do not think that your heart can stand the shock of such awesome ugliness. But you do not need to worry about your heart. You cannot move.

The End

You walk to the right and cross over a bridge. When you reach the other side, you hear a scream.

"Help me!" says a voice.

You look around, but you see nothing except an extraordinary tree by the side of the road.

"Where are you?" you call out.

"I've been made a prisoner in the Monkey Puzzle tree!" the voice says. "It's the Leprechaun. He did it to me because I wouldn't laugh at his jokes."

"I'll help if I can," you say. "But who are you?"

"I am a Pooka," says the voice. "An invisible rabbit. And if you help me, I will give you the power to be invisible."

If you go to the Leprechaun and try to convince him to free the Pooka, turn to page 108.

If you do not like the idea of dealing with something invisible, turn to page 109.

The road is lonely and desolate, and the sun is hot. You round the bend in the path and are suddenly confronted with a blinding, dazzling light.

At the same time, you hear a small voice say, "Hi, stranger. Come say hello."

If you think that this is a trick and want to go back to the other road, turn to page 82.

If you investigate the voice and the light, turn to page 110.

You tell Nyk that you want to go home now.

"Of course," says Nyk. "I'll show you the way."

You swim to the surface on Nyk's back and step onto the land.

You look down at the scale in your hand. You are saddened and disappointed to see that the scale has turned to a dull gray powder.

"What happened?"

"Every creature in nature has a way of protecting itself. You thought that you were carrying proof that Nessie exists." Nyk pauses. "But you never stopped to think of what would happen to her if you were to reveal the secret of where she lives. Soon, she would be hunted and trapped and put on exhibit in some terribly confining zoo. Nessie's scales turn to powder when they are touched by light, so that no one will ever have proof of her existence. It would kill Nessie to become a prisoner."

"I wish I had thought of that before I left your kingdom."

Nyk nods in understanding. "Come. I will show you the way home."

The End

"Would you like to stay with me for a while?" Nessie asks.

"I'd love to!" you answer. You cannot imagine anything more wonderful than to learn more about the Loch Ness monster. How exciting it will be to share your knowledge and experience with your parents and friends. You tell Nessie that everyone will envy you when they hear about what you have been doing.

"Oh," Nessie says. "If you stay, you must never tell anyone that we have met. You must promise me that."

"But why?"

"Because if people knew where and how I live, they would capture me. If I were forced to live in a zoo, I would die of a broken heart. Freedom is as important to me as food. Without freedom, I could not survive." She pauses. "Promise that you will never reveal what you know about me. My life depends on your ability to keep this secret."

"I promise," you say. And you know that for the remainder of your days you will be enriched with the remembrance of your experience, and frustrated by your promise to keep this extraordinary secret.

The End

Before leaving the castle, Nyk grabs the bugle that is hanging near the moat. When you are a safe distance away from the castle, he blows his emergency call. Soon the sea around you is filled with millions of creatures, large and small.

Nyk explains the situation to his subjects, and then he outlines his plan.

Only the smallest creatures of the sea return to the castle. Nyk opens the door, and millions of tiny fish, hermit crabs, and eels swarm over the monster.

"Hey, stupid! You can't get us!" they taunt. "Hey, clumsy! You couldn't catch a fish in a barrel!" they yell at the Octopus.

(continued on page 88)

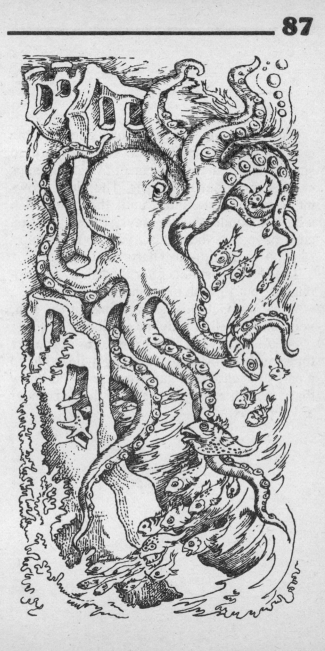

With first one tentacle, then another, the monster tries to grab them. But they are so small that the mere movement of his tentacles sweeps them out of danger. The giant grows more and more frantic, until the tiniest fish with the loudest voice says, "Your suction cups have lost their suck, you no-neck monster!" And the little fish darts out the door.

The Octopus shoots after the fish by jet propulsion, but the fish hides in the seaweed.

While the Octopus is searching for the fish, you and Nyk slip inside the castle.

Then Nyk invites all the creatures of the sea for a royal celebration. You are privileged to be a part of such a rare gathering, and you know that you will remember this for the remainder of your days.

The End

First, you tie your mirrorlike shield to your foot with a rope. Then, you float on your back in front of the castle door, holding out the shield so that when the Octopus looks out he will see his reflection.

Cautiously, Nyk opens the door. The Octopus is startled when he sees his reflection. He thinks that he is seeing another creature like himself. He reaches out toward his own image, but you slowly kick your feet and back away. The Octopus follows as you move farther and farther away from the castle.

When you see Nyk slip inside the castle, you untie the shield and watch as it drifts to the bottom of the sea. The Octopus follows the shield, and you swim quickly back to the castle.

"You have saved my castle," Nyk says with gratitude. "I am sorry you had to give up your shield."

"It was a small price to pay in exchange for all the new worlds you are showing me," you answer. "This has been the most extraordinary experience of my life."

The End

You go back the way you came, and soon you reach the iron fence.

In the distance, across a huge field, you can see the Cyclops. He has left the gold unguarded.

You run around the fence toward the gold, but the Cyclops sees you. With one enormous step, he crosses the field. Then he bends down and picks you up between his thumb and forefinger.

"You're a cute little animal," says the Cyclops. "I've never seen one like you before. I think I'll keep you for a pet." Then he carefully places you in a cage with a cup of water and a bowl of mush.

The End

You head west toward the Lake of Boiling Blood.

Less than a mile down the path, you are startled to see a huge giant sitting on the ground. This monster has the two ugliest eyes you have ever seen. In fact, his whole face is perfectly hideous.

Then you notice that he is weeping.

You cup your hands around your mouth and yell, "Are you all right?"

The giant looks down at you. He is obviously quite surprised. "No Earthling has ever spoken to Balan before," he bellows in as soft a voice as he can manage. "Everyone is afraid of me. And, since you ask the question, the answer is, no. I am not all right. I have this splinter in my toe. It is so small that I cannot get hold of it with my fingers," Balan says.

"Let me take a look," you say; you grab a tuft of hair on his gigantic big toe and pull yourself onto his foot. Then you crawl on hands and knees to the end of his pinkie toe. The splinter is huge, the size of a broom handle.

You grab the splinter and tug with all your might.

(continued on page 92)

You pull and pull, and suddenly you fall backward, the splinter in your arms.

"You did it!" the giant says. "What favor may I do for you in return?"

"I am trying to get to the Bower of Bliss, but I do not know how to cross the Lake of Boiling Blood."

"Oh," says Balan. "I'll be glad to help you."

The giant picks you up and holds you securely in his arms. Leaning forward, he takes a running start. Then, with an enormous leap, he jumps over the bright red lake that is bubbling below you.

As he lands on the far shore, the impact of the landing makes the earth tremble. Buildings quiver and collapse; hillsides crumble.

"Earthquake! Earthquake!" the people cry as they run in terror.

"I've done it again!" weeps the giant. "Every time I try to help, I mess up! I can't do anything right." Then he sits down and puts his hands over his face in despair.

If you try to soothe the giant's sadness, turn to page 111.

If you run after the people and try to convince them that this is a good giant, turn to page 112.

Cautiously, you reach inside the trap, sweeping your hand around to feel for whatever is there.

"Gotcha!" says a hideous voice as he grabs your hand.

With one powerful jerk, you are pulled down into the awful darkness.

The End

The Ogre hands you a flute. One of the Pixies shows you how to play it.

You try to play, but all that comes out is a horrible squeak. You blow again. But this time, the sound is even worse.

"Stop!" yells the Ogre as he reaches for you. "Let's hope that you taste better than you play!"

The End

"Dance?" the Ogre says, dumbfounded. "You want to teach me to dance?"

You nod, too frightened to speak.

"So do it!" he says. "Play for us!" he orders the Pixies.

The music begins, and you show the Ogre the steps. Once he has learned them, you direct the Pixies to play faster and faster. You continue to dance, urging the clumsy Ogre on.

(continued on page 96)

"Slow down!" he yells at the Pixies.

But you indicate to the Pixies that they should play even faster.

Faster and faster the music goes as the Ogre tries in vain to keep up. You see that he is exhausted, and you dance nimbly toward the flute players.

(continued on page 97)

Suddenly, there is a resounding crash as the Ogre falls, exhausted, to the floor. Soon he is sound asleep.

Quickly, you unchain the Pixies. They whisper their thanks to you.

"As soon as we escape," the Pixies say, "we will lead you home again."

The End

Joining hands with your tiny partners, you dance around the flickering fires in a joyful celebration of the coming of the light.

You have been dancing for hours when, suddenly, there is a huge explosion of thunder. Then torrents of rain drown the fires and plunge the world into total darkness. The Elves are very frightened.

Then the King of the Elves, who is standing next to you, explains, "The Genie has caused the rain. He has deliberately ruined our festival."

All around you, you can hear the Elves trying frantically to light the fires. But it is no use. Everything is too wet.

(continued on page 99)

"Years ago," continues the King of the Elves, "the Genie stole one of our Elf children. We banished him from the Land of Light forever. Now he is putting out our fires in revenge. If we cannot rekindle the fires, we will live forever in darkness. We are helpless in the dark," he explains. "Since you are larger than we, perhaps you can save us. Will you try?"

You tell him that you will.

"Wear this ring," says the King. "Its magic will grant you one wish . . . but only when your life is threatened. Choose your wish wisely, for there is no recalling it."

If you ask the Roc to take you to the Genie, turn to page 114.

If you seek out the South Wind in hope that he can help you, turn to page 115.

You move away from the bonfires toward a shadowy light in the distance.

"Beware of Grendel," calls one of the Elves.

If I can conquer a Hydra, I can certainly take care of a Grendel, you think.

As you walk toward the murky light, suddenly a huge silhouette blocks your way. You look up and see a ferocious giant.

"Who are you?" you ask, terrified.

"I am Grendel," the giant says.

"What do you do?"

"I stalk the boundaries of the night. And I collect people who intrude upon my territory," he answers as he reaches out and puts you in his pocket.

"Hi there," says a tiny voice curled up next to you in the bottom of the pocket. "Don't worry about him. He always forgets we're here. When he goes to sleep, we creep out and carry on our business. Would you please move over just a little bit so I can stretch my legs."

The End

The monster has the head of a woman. But her body is that of a lion. From her back, two wings sprout.

There is a surprising gentleness about this monster and a peaceful quality to this place. Birds sing sweetly. The air is crystal clear. You would like to stay here for a long time.

As if she can read your thoughts, the monster says, "Welcome to the Land of the Sphinx. You may stay here as long as you wish if you can guess the answer to my riddle:

"What goes on four feet, two feet, and three;
But the more feet it goes on, the weaker it be?"

If you think the answer to this riddle is an insect that changes into different shapes during its life cycle, turn to page 116.

If you think the answer to this is a human being, turn to page 117.

As the Fafner comes straight at you, you have an idea. You hold your shield in front of you and begin to swing it slowly back and forth, back and forth. You watch as the dragon's eyes follow every movement of the shield. Soon he is hypnotized and sound asleep.

Quickly, you step forward and slay the dragon with your sword. As fast as you can, you pull his teeth and put them in your bag.

Then you enter the foul-smelling lair and carry out three bags of gold.

(continued on page 103)

You run immediately to the Leprechaun's home.

When you arrive, a great cheer of gratitude fills the air.

"At last!" says the Leprechaun. "We have the dragon's teeth to sow. Finally, we can defend ourselves against the Witches. You are truly a hero. We shall celebrate your deeds for as long as we live. And, as you know, we live for hundreds of years."

The End

You run to the tree and begin to climb, while the Fafner lumbers after you. Thank goodness the dragon is slow and clumsy, you think. He'll never catch me.

(continued on page 105)

You climb onto a branch. Beneath you, the Fafner snorts. You try to hold out your shield for protection, but in doing so you lose your balance and drop the shield.

The Fafner does not even notice. He raises himself clumsily on his hind legs and spews his venom directly at you.

The End

You turn toward the rats. They must be after the egg, you think. You hold the egg up over your head and get ready to throw it at them.

Suddenly, the rats stop as if a magical barrier has risen between you and your enemy.

An eerie glow is cast over the vermin. They squirm and squeal.

You back away slowly as you hold the magical Serpent's Egg in front of you.

This is only the beginning, you think. *I have the power now to create strange and wonderful happenings. I must use this power wisely.*

The End

Clutching the egg with both hands, you begin to run. You can hear the rats close behind you. Panicked, you increase your pace.

You are so frightened of being overrun by a pack of angry rats that you do not watch where you are going. You trip over a branch in the path and fall.

The Serpent's Egg slips from your grasp and crashes to the ground. It shatters into a million pieces.

You weep with sadness because you know that all the magic, all the power you longed for has been destroyed.

The End

The Leprechaun lives among the roots of an old apple tree. You go to the tree and get down on your hands and knees.

You are about to call out when a tiny voice says, "You're invading my privacy! Go away from here!"

"Not until you talk to me about the Pooka," you say.

"All right," says the little man. "But first I shall ask you some riddles."

If you tell the Leprechaun that you did not come to listen to riddles, turn to page 118.

If you listen to the riddles, turn to page 119.

You continue your way down the road. Behind you, you hear the voice calling out once more for help. But invisibility frightens you too much to answer the plea.

You come to another fork in the road. To the right, the path is marked "Land of Good Deeds." To the left, the path is marked "Land of Nothingness."

You start down the right path, but you are stopped by an unknown force. You will not be allowed to travel on that path.

Sadly, you turn to the left.

The End

Squinting your eyes so that the glare will not hurt them, you move toward the light. You discover that the intense rays are coming from a simple mirror.

Everything about the mirror is ordinary, except there is a funny little man staring at you from inside the glass. You look around, but there is no one else there. You are alone.

"That's right," says the little man. "I *am* inside the mirror. Your imagination is not playing tricks on you."

"But how did you get there?" you ask.

"A Witch cast a spell on me centuries ago. She was jealous because I am the Wizard of the Wind and I can fly. Her flight permission had been taken from her because she abused the privilege. She was so jealous that she trapped me in this mirror."

"How can I help you?" you ask.

"Anything is worth a try," says the Wizard. "I'm getting bored in here."

If you break the mirror, turn to page 120.

If you think that it might be dangerous to break the mirror, turn to page 122.

You climb up Balan's leg and sit on his bent knee so that you can talk with him.

"Hey, Balan," you say as you look at the collapsed buildings around you. "I have an idea." You talk to him for a while, explaining your plan. When he finally stops crying, he reaches over to the building nearest him and starts to put it back together.

"You're very artistic," you say to Balan, as he adds an indoor garden to one building. Then he builds a fanciful tower on a very ordinary home, because he knows that the child who lives there will have fun in a tower.

By the end of the morning, the people begin to return to their homes. They are delighted to see the changes that have taken place.

"Balan did it all!" you say. "Isn't he terrific?"

Then you explain to the people in the Bower of Bliss about the inhabitants of the arid land.

At first, the Bower-of-Bliss people have trouble understanding about hunger and starvation. They have never been hungry themselves. But after you describe the terrible conditions in the arid land, they devise a plan to help their unfortunate neighbors.

Proud of your successful mission, you and Balan leave the Bower of Bliss.

The End

You run after the people and—one by one—you calm them down so that you can talk to them.

"First of all," you say, "the giant did not intend to destroy your homes, and I am certain that he can rebuild them in no time at all. So please put your minds at rest about that.

"Now . . . to continue. We have a problem. The people of the arid land are starving."

"Nobody starves! Just look around you!" one man says. "How foolish even to think that!"

"It is true," you say. "They have no food; they have no water."

"How terrible," says a woman. "We must help them. We will send them food every week."

"It is important to feed them. But that does not mean you must send them food forever. What they need most of all is water," you explain. "Then the arid land will bloom, just like the Bower of Bliss.

(continued on page 113)

"We can get Balan to lay a pipeline for water from here, across the Lake of Boiling Blood, and into the arid land. Then the people will be able to irrigate and plant and harvest the fruits of their labor. If you share your water with them, you will give them life."

A great cheer goes up as the crowd gathers around to praise you for your excellent plan. Congratulations. You have saved the people of the arid land.

The End

The Roc picks you up in his talons, and once again you are flying. Higher and higher you go, until the great bird sets you down at the edge of a cave at the top of a mountain.

Plumes of smoke drift from the cave as you step inside.

"How dare you invade my domain without my permission!" roars a voice. Then you see a shining sword swooping toward you.

If you think you can get out of this difficult situation without using up your one wish, turn to page 123.

If you use your magic ring now to save your life, turn to page 124.

The Roc takes you to where the South Wind lives and sets you down gently in a field of clover.

"Who is this Earthling who has the audacity to enter the land where the South Wind lives?" puffs a voice.

"It is only I," you start to explain.

But the wind is in no mood for explanations. He starts to blow up a terrible gale. You feel yourself being lifted off your feet and blown, helter-skelter, into the sky.

If you use the ring's wish now to save your life, turn to page 125.

If you save your wish for later, turn to page 126.

"An insect?" you ask.

"An insect!" says the Sphinx. "Don't be ridiculous!" She pauses for a moment and then says, "Go now from this land. From this moment forward, you are banished forever."

A haunting sadness steals through you as you turn and walk toward a world of ordinary happenings.

The End

"A human being?" you ask, uncertain of your answer.

"Of course," the Sphinx says. "When you are a baby, you crawl on all fours. As a man or a woman, you walk upright on two legs. But when you are old and weak, you must walk with a cane."

The Sphinx smiles, and the light of her pleasure fills you with warmth.

"You may stay here as long as you like, and you may return as often as you wish. You are always welcome here in the Land of the Sphinx."

The End

"What!" says the Leprechaun. "You will not listen to my riddles? If you do not listen to riddles, that means that you do not like to laugh. And if you do not like to laugh, then you should be put where you cannot mar people's lives with your gloom."

In the blink of an eye, you find yourself perched on a branch of the Monkey Puzzle tree.

"What? You, too?" says the Pooka.

The End

"What's the best way to catch a squirrel?" asks the Leprechaun.

"I don't know," you say.

"Climb up a tree and act like a nut!" the Leprechaun answers, laughing hysterically.

You giggle.

"What's gray, has big ears, four legs, and a trunk?"

"An elephant," you say.

"Nope. A mouse on vacation," the Leprechaun says.

You laugh hysterically.

"What does a monster do when he loses a hand?"

"I don't know," you say.

"He goes to a second-hand store," says the Leprechaun, rolling on the ground with mirth. You laugh so hard that you fall on the ground.

When both of you finally stop laughing, the Leprechaun says that you are the best audience he has ever had and that he will reward you with any wish in the world.

If you wish for the pot of gold at the end of the rainbow, turn to page 127.

If you wish for the Pooka's freedom from the Monkey Puzzle tree, turn to page 128.

You pick up a rock and smash it into the mirror. There is a huge crash, but the glass does not fall apart. Instead, it cracks into hundreds of tiny sections.

"Woe is me!" says the Wizard. You look into the mirror and see seven eyes, twenty-three arms and legs. Hands and pointed shoes are everywhere.

"Now look at me," the Wizard cries. "I'm still trapped, and I'm in crazy pieces, too. The only hope now is for you to talk to the Witch."

(continued on page 121)

"Close your eyes and turn three times," says the Wizard.

You do as the Wizard says. When you open your eyes, you are sitting beneath a strange tree with blue leaves.

You feel hungry, but there is nothing to eat; so, you take a piece of bubble gum out of your pocket and begin to chew.

"Who are you?" asks a Witch who appears out of nowhere.

"Who, me?" you ask.

"Yes, indeed, my pretty." The Witch looks at you in a strange way. "What are you eating?" she asks.

"Bubble gum," you answer.

"There is no such thing," says the Witch. "If there were, I would have it."

"Well, there is, and you don't," you say.

Turn to page 129.

"I am afraid that if I break the mirror, you might break into pieces, too," you say. "Didn't the Witch tell you anything at all that might help?"

"The only thing the old biddy told me was some sort of stupid riddle. Then she left."

"Well, what was the riddle?" you ask.

> "You're trapped forever in the looking glass.
> Your only freedom is black, alas."

If you tell the Wizard that you will wait until the darkest part of the night to see if there is a solution hiding in the blackness, turn to page 131.

If you look around for something else that is black, turn to page 132.

You think that you can duck the sword and then talk to the Genie. But you are wrong.

The End

You rub the ring and say out loud, "May the Genie's sword crumble into thousands of pieces!"

And the sword does just that.

"I'm impressed," says the Genie as he looks at the pieces of sword lying on the floor. "Your magic is powerful."

"Not so powerful as the magic I shall use if you do not remove the rain from the Land of Light," you reply, hoping the Genie does not know about rings that grant only one wish. "Do you want me to show you?" you ask in the bravest voice you can manage.

"After the sword, I do not have any desire to see any more of your magic," the Genie replies. "I shall remove the curse of the rain, just as you wish. Now, go from here before I change my mind."

You step outside, and the Roc is waiting for you.

The End

You rub the ring and say out loud, "I wish to remain in one place until I finish with the wind."

Suddenly you are deposited on the ground. The wind continues to blow, but you do not move.

"Ha ha! You can't get me!" you taunt the wind. And he blows harder and longer in his anger. All the while, you know that the hot South Wind is also blowing across the Land of Light and drying out the kindling wood.

You laugh at the wind, and he continues to blow. You keep on taunting him until you are certain that the Land of Light is dry. And then you signal for the Roc to carry you back so that you can once again join the Elves in their celebration of light.

The End

You feel yourself flying. You love the swooshing and drifting and turning, and you forget for a moment why it is you came to the South Wind.

As you are soaring through the air, caring for nothing except the sensation of flight, your ring blows off your finger. You see the ring disappearing into space, and you know that soon you will follow it into the void.

The End

"Ah!" says the Leprechaun. "The pot of gold. That's easy. Just travel over the next hill, and you will find that you are as high as the top of the rainbow's arc. All you have to do is climb on and slide to the bottom."

You do exactly as the Leprechaun says. You are exhilarated by the great swooshing slide through a kaleidoscope of endlessly changing colors.

You float gently to the bottom and land right next to an enormous pot of gold. You are thrilled when you think of all the things you will do with the gold.

Taking the pot, you step onto the rainbow and begin to climb back. But the rainbow is like greased glass, and you keep sliding back to the bottom.

You have the gold, but you have nowhere and no way to use it. You are trapped by your own wish.

The End

By the time you return to the Monkey Puzzle tree, the Pooka is free. At least that's what he tells you. You cannot see him, of course, because a Pooka remains invisible forever.

After he thanks you, the Pooka says, "Take this medallion." Right in front of you, a gold medallion, hanging from a platinum chain, dangles in midair.

You take the necklace and slip it on.

"Henceforth, for the rest of your life," says the Pooka, "whenever you rub this medallion, you will become invisible. If you misuse the magic, the medallion will become just another ordinary necklace. But if you use it wisely, the magic shall remain with you for the remainder of your days."

The End

You mash the gum between your tongue and the roof of your mouth. Then you blow a huge bubble.

"I must have that!" cries the Witch.

"But you can't," you say nonchalantly.

"I *must* have it," she insists.

"It's not really that big a deal," you answer; then you blow an even bigger bubble.

"Well, if it's not a big deal, then give it to me."

"It belongs to me," you reply.

"I must have it!" begs the Witch. "Anything. I'll trade anything for it."

"Gee . . . I don't know," you answer reluctantly.

"Anything!"

"Anything?"

"I promise."

"Then free the Wizard from the mirror."

(continued on page 130)

"I'll free the Wizard as soon as you give me the bubble stuff."

"Oh, no," you reply. "Free the Wizard first."

"All right," she says, and she mumbles some crazy jumbled words. Suddenly, the Wizard is standing beside you.

"How can I thank you?" he says. "You have saved me from a life of imprisonment."

"Now, give it to me," the Witch says.

You reach into your pocket and take out the remaining sticks of gum in the pack. But the Witch cries at you with an impatient voice, "Don't try to trick me. I want that bubble stuff right this instant!" And she puts the palm of her hand under your mouth.

Very obligingly, you smile and say, "As you wish." And then you spit the piece of gum into her waiting and eager hand.

The End

By midnight, everything is pitch black. You watch for a clue that might help you solve the riddle.

"Who are you?" says a cackling, wicked voice from out of the dark.

You do not answer.

"Whoever you are, you must be trying to break my spell. Well, I'll show you about spells," says the Witch.

When dawn breaks and the land is light once more, you look around. Standing next to you is the Wizard. You have become his companion in the mirror.

The End

You look around for something black. But you see nothing that might help free the Wizard.

You walk around the mirror three times. The third time around, you notice that the back of the mirror itself is black. *How stupid of me!* you think.

You search until you find a sharp rock. Then you begin to scrape. The black paint comes off easily, and soon the Wizard of the Wind steps out of the mirror.

(continued on page 133)

"You have saved my life," he says, embracing you. "I wish to give you a reward for your help."

"Can you teach me to fly?" you ask.

"Can I?" he answers. "That's my specialty. It takes practice, of course."

"Is it a magic spell?"

"No. It is a form of self-hypnosis."

You listen carefully as the Wizard tells you how to place your mind in a trance. You feel your body grow lighter and lighter, until you lift off the ground. Soon you are soaring with the eagles. Reluctantly, you return to earth so that you can thank the Wizard.

"It was wonderful," you say. "I'm sorry it is over."

"But it's not!" says the Wizard. "If you discipline yourself, you may be the possessor of this gift for the remainder of your life. Wherever you go, whatever you do, just use this method of hypnosis, and the gift of flight is yours."

You lean over and hug the Wizard. And then you take off for the long and wondrous flight home.

The End